HARRIET ZIEFERT

WHAT IS PART THIS, PART THAT?

illustrations by
TOM SLAUGHTER

BLUE APPLE

Just like a bee is part BUZZ
and part STING,

a rap song
is part
TALK
and part
SING.

Is this glass part
EMPTY,
or is it part
FULL?

Is this swing
part
PUSH,

or is it part
PULL?

Steps
in a staircase
are part
DOWN
and part
UP.

Where's the fruit?

It's in the dish that's part

PLATE

and part

CUP.

Daddy's pajamas
are part
BOTTOM,

part
TOP.

Riding in traffic is part GO and part STOP.
TAXI

A silvery seaplane
is part
FLY

and part
FLOAT.

These cozy slippers
are part

SOCK

and part SHOE.

What happens when you mix

part YELLOW,

part BLUE?

This pretty mermaid is part FISH
and part GIRL.

What's found in the sea that's part
SHELL
and part
PEARL?

A penguin's tuxedo is part

BLACK

and part

WHITE.

Here is a ride
that's part

FUN

and part

FRIGHT!

When you talk
to a friend,
it's part
LISTEN
and part
SAY.

What time
of day
is part

WASH

and part

PLAY?

A rocking chair goes part **BACK**

and part **FORTH.**

When you stand on the equator,
you're part SOUTH and part NORTH.

This yellow
zipper
is part

UP

and part

DOWN.

nimal
TE
and part
BROWN?

nimal
TE
and part
BROWN?

What farm animal

is part

WHITE

and part

BROWN?

Just like
a candle
is part

WAX

and part

WICK,

what spooky night

is part

TREAT

and part

TRICK?

Take a ride on a carousel.
It's part
GO-ROUND
and part
MERRY!

Make a
fruit smoothie.
It's part
MILK

and part
BERRY.

Add two
straws—
one red and
one blue.

Guess what comes next?

Part for
ME...
part for
YOU!

Put on your thinking cap.
Use all of your smarts!

A play is part REAL and part "LET'S PRETEND."

A secret's part WHISPER and part KEEPING MUM.

A snail is part SOFT, the other part SHELL.

Pink is part RED and also part WHITE.

A wave is part "LOOK AT ME" and part "HOWDY DO!"

School is part WORK and part FUN, of course!

Vacation days are part FAST, part WAY-TOO-SLOW.

A hug is part SQUEEZE and also part HOLD.

A hide-and-seek game is part QUIET, part BOO.

A panda is part WHITE and part BLACK.

Can you guess the answers from both of the parts?

What exercise is part STRETCH and part BEND?

What musical instrument is part CYMBAL, part DRUM?

A runny nose? Are you part SICK or are you part WELL?

What small animal is part LICK and part BITE?

What beaked animal is part SWOOP and part "WHOOO?"

What farm animal is part DONKEY and also part HORSE?

What's the word that means part YES and part NO?

What's the temperature when it's part HOT and part COLD?

Do you know someone who's part COO and part POO?

What do you read that's part FRONT and part BACK?

For Charlie and Lucy—
part Hochhauser, part Ziefert
—HZ

For the brothers B. C. J.
—TS

Text copyright © 2013 by Harriet Ziefert
Illustrations copyright © 2013 by Tom Slaughter
All rights reserved / CIP data is available.
Published in the United States 2013 by

Blue Apple Books
515 Valley Street, Maplewood, NJ 07040
www.blueapplebooks.com
First Edition 05/13 Printed in China
ISBN: 978-1-60905-309-3

10 9 8 7 6 5 4 3 2 1

Just like dancing is part step
and part swing,
When you put parts together,
you get a new thing!

Put on your thinking cap.
Use all of your smarts!
Follow along and imagine
both of the parts.